A RAILWAY
ABC
BY JACK TOWNEND

V&A Publishing

First published in 1942
This edition published by
V&A Publishing, 2015

V&A Publishing
Victoria and Albert Museum
South Kensington
London SW7 2RL
www.vandapublishing.com

Distributed in North America by
Abrams Books for Yound Readers,
an imprint of ABRAMS

Jack Townend (1918–2005) was an English
artist and illustrator. *A Railway ABC* is in
the collection of the Victoria and Albert
Museum's National Art Library, which
includes over 100,000 children's books.

V&A Publishing

Supporting the world's leading
museum of art and design,
the Victoria and Albert
Museum, London

ISBN 978 1 85177 844 7

Library of Congress Control Number
2014946846

10 9 8 7 6 5 4 3 2 1
2018 2017 2016 2015

A catalogue record for this book is
available from the British Library.

Printed in China

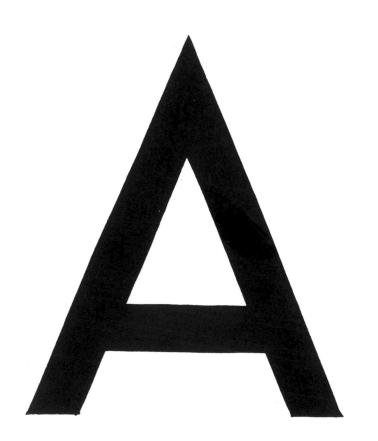

for
ALL CLEAR
as the
signal goes
down

for the
BUFFERS
which sit
there
and frown

for the
COACHES
in which
we all
ride

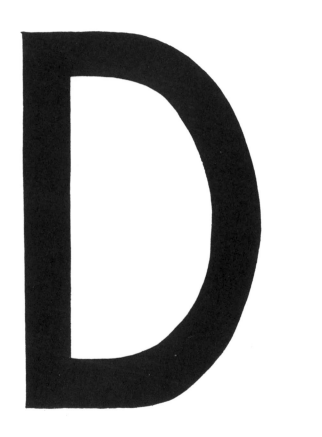

for the
DRIVER
the engine's
his pride

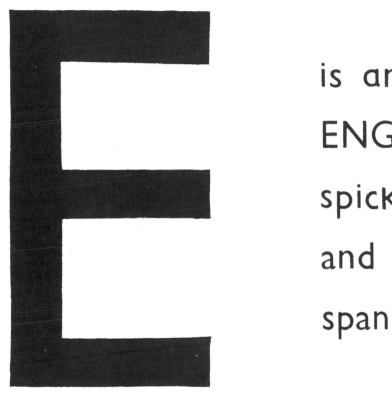

is an
ENGINE
spick
and
span

for the
FIREMAN
whose
name
is Dan

for the
GUARD
as his
whistle
he blows

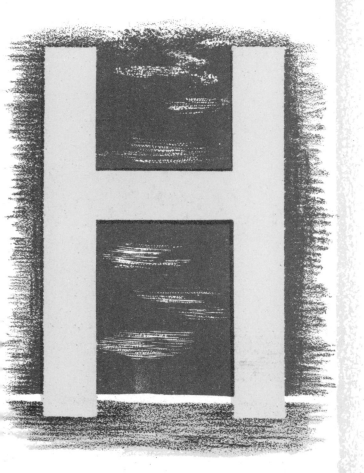

is the
HOPPER
through which
the coal
goes

the

INSPECTOR

who stands

at the

gate

for the
JUNCTION
here's
where
we wait

for the

KITCHEN

with pans

all

a-glow

for the
LAMPS
which
stand in
a row

is the
MAIL
which is
urgent
indeed

is a

NIGHT-TRAIN

running

at

speed

is the
OLD MAN
who
works on
the line

for the

PORTER

he's

sturdy

and fine

is the
QUEUE
for the
train which
is late

for the
RAILS
some curved
and
some straight

 for the
SIGNALS
which say
" Stop "
or " Go "

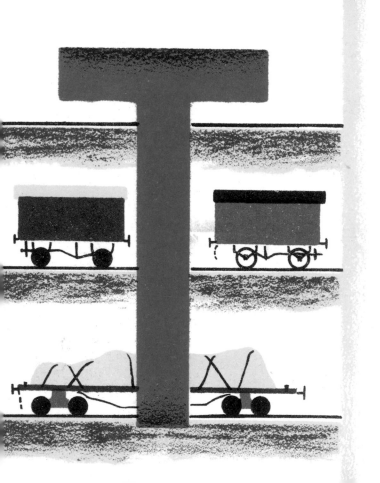

for the
TRUCKS
some high
and
some low

the

UMBRELLA

left

by

Aunt Sally

is the
VIADUCT
which
crosses
the valley

W the
WATER-TANK,
where
the engines
drink

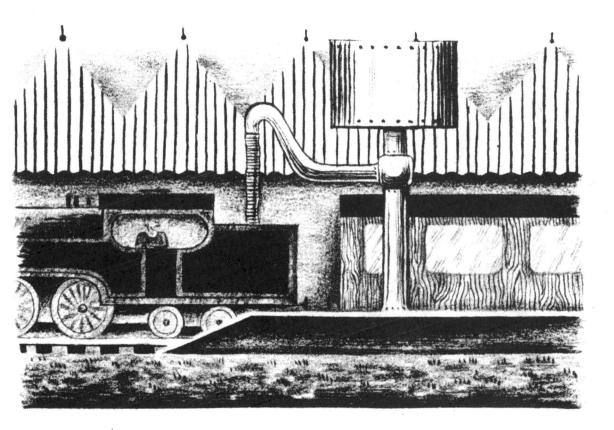

is the
CROSSING
where the
red light
blinks

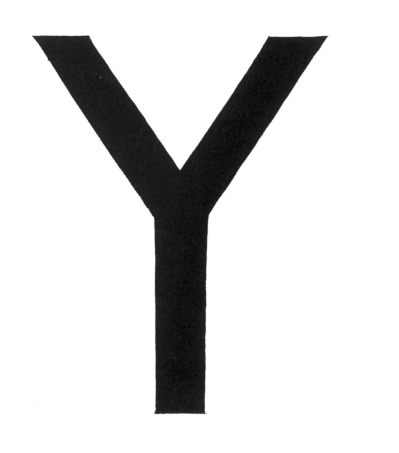

is for

YORK

a very

big

Station

is the
ZOO
which
is our
destination

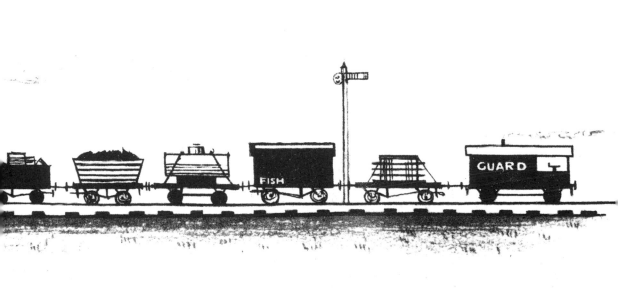

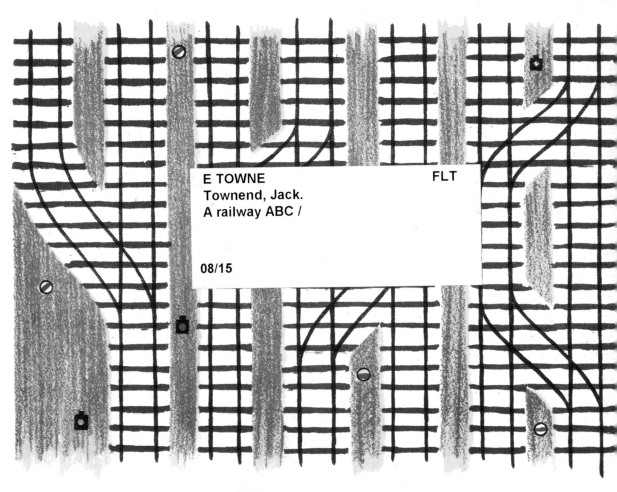

E TOWNE   FLT
Townend, Jack.
A railway ABC /

08/15